I0669805

Sydney Rosenfeld

Rosemi Shell

Sydney Rosenfeld

Rosemi Shell

ISBN/EAN: 9783337389727

Printed in Europe, USA, Canada, Australia, Japan

Cover: Foto ©Andreas Hilbeck / pixelio.de

More available books at **www.hansebooks.com**

DE WITT'S ACTING PLAYS.

(Number 195.)

ROSEMI SHELL.

A TRAVESTY,

FOUNDED ON THE MACKAYE-BLUM MELODRAMA OF THE UNION
SQUARE THEATRE, NEW YORK, "ROSE MICHEL" (PLAYED
DURING THE SEASON OF 1875 AND 1876.)

By SYDNEY ROSENFELD,

Author of "Off the Stage," "Mr. X," "Sweet Sixteen," "Success" (founded on Paul Lindau's "Ein Erfolg"), etc.; and Adapter of "Money and Brains" (De Witt's "Ultimo"), "High C," "On Bread and Water," etc., etc.

TO WHICH ARE ADDED,

A description of the Costumes—Synopsis of the Piece—Cast of the Characters
—Entrances and Exits—Relative Positions of the Performers on
the Stage, and the whole of the Stage Business.

AUTHOR'S EDITION.

ALL ACTING RIGHTS RESERVED.

New-York:

ROBERT M. DE WITT, PUBLISHER,

No. 33 Rose Street.

DE WITT'S HALF-DIME MUSIC

OF THE BEST SONGS FOR VOICE AND PIANO.

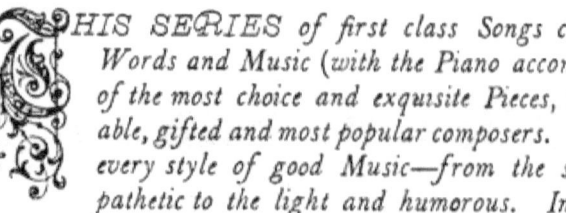 THIS SERIES of first class Songs contains the Words and Music (*with the Piano accompaniment*) of the most choice and exquisite Pieces, by the most able, gifted and most popular composers. It contains every style of good Music—from the solemn and pathetic to the light and humorous. In brief, this collection is a complete Musical Library in itself, both of VOCAL AND PIANO-FORTE MUSIC. It is printed from new, clear, distinct, elegant Music Type, on fine white paper, made expressly for this Series, and is published at the low price of FIVE CENTS.

Remember, EACH NUMBER CONTAINS A COMPLETE PIECE OF MUSIC, *beautifully printed on Sheet Music Paper.*

Any Twenty Pieces mailed on receipt of One Dollar, postage paid.

☞ *PLEASE ORDER BY THE NUMBERS.* ☜

Address,　　　　　　　　　　R. M. DE WITT, Publisher,

33 Rose Street, N. Y.

SENTIMENTAL SONGS AND BALLADS.

ROSEMI SHELL;

OR,

MY DAUGHTER! OH! MY DAUGHTER.

A NEW AND ORIGINAL EMOTIONAL, SENSATIONAL, GROTESQUE INCIDENTAL,
TRAGICAL, MAGICAL, FARCICAL, MUSICAL, CONTEMPORANEOUSLY NON-
SENSICAL "WHAT YOU MAY NAME IT;" EXECUTED WITH MAL-
ICE AFORETHOUGHT, AND BASELY BASED UPON THE *STEELE-
BLUM* MELODRAMATIC SUCCESS OF UNION SQUARE.

By SYDNEY ROSENFELD,

*Author of "Off the Stage," "Mr. X," "Sweet Sixteen," "Success" (founded on Paul
Lindau's "Ein Erfolg"), etc.; and Adapter of "Money and Brains" (De
Witt's "Ultimo"), "High C," "On Bread and Water," etc., etc.*

AS FIRST PERFORMED AT THE EAGLE THEATRE, NEW YORK,
JANUARY, 1876.

TO WHICH ARE ADDED,

A DESCRIPTION OF THE COSTUMES—CAST OF THE CHARACTERS—SYNOP-
SIS OF THE PIECE—ENTRANCES AND EXITS—RELATIVE POSI-
TIONS OF THE PERFORMERS ON THE STAGE, AND THE
WHOLE OF THE STAGE BUSINESS.

AUTHOR'S EDITION.

ALL ACTING RIGHTS RESERVED.

———— ————

NEW YORK:
ROBERT M. DE WITT, PUBLISHER,
No. 33 ROSE STREET.
[BETWEEN DUANE AND FRANKFORT STREETS.]

To

THE DISTINGUISHED ARTIST AND MANAGER,

MATT MORGAN,

TO WHOSE GENEROUS FRIENDSHIP I OWE THE FIRST INTRODUCTION OF MY

PLAY TO THE THEATRE

WHERE ITS MERIT WAS RECOGNIZED, I GRATEFULLY DEDICATE THIS TRAVESTY,

WITH MANY AND SINCERE WELL-WISHES.

SYDNEY ROSENFELD.

SOLID CAST OF CHARACTERS.

(*Cast Iron-ically.*)

As performed at the Eagle Theatre,
New York, Jan., 1876.

Count de Ferny (the necessary *Thorne* to every *Rose*; a gallant *mister*, but a victim to *Ey-tinge* of cruel *mystery*)...Mr. LARRY TOOLEY.

Baron de Bestfille (a *roué*, who gets his *best fille* of life before the play begins, but has cause to *roué 't* before it is over)......Mr. JAS. F. CROSSEN.

Baron de Morris-and-Essex (*Prefect of the Seine, perfectly inseine*, who gets himself into a *Parselle* of difficulties by *managing* too many *stages* at once)......Mr. JAMES BRADLEY.

Piermi Shell (a miserly barkeeper, a fearful scamp; in fact, as you will find *out* if you stay *in* long enough and *live* to see it, a villain of the deepest *die*)......Mr. G. H. MACDERMOTT.

Mule-in-Hay, with a cold in the head (his servant, called the *Sneezer*, because that's *Sneezer* way to call him)......Mr. JOHN WILD.

Andrew (a nice little fellow for a cent, very fond of "*spoon*," but not of the bitter *dose* that often comes with it)......Miss LOUISE FRANKLIN.

Baroness de Bestfille (supposed to be married to the Baron, and retired from the *humdrum* of life, though *why'f* she's the Baron's *wife* she shouldn't live with him is a *con-humdrum*)......Miss MARIE GORENFLO.

Rosemi Shell (the wife of a husband and the mother of a daughter, who suffers with violent emotion and the *new Delsarte* system—though the last is a *noodle sort* of system to suffer with and enough to MACKAYE man sweat)......Mr. G. K. FORTESCUE.

Susie (the daughter, oh, the daughter, who clings to her lover with *un-Varian* devotion)......Miss MILLIE COOKE.

Supers, White Guards and Black Guards.

SCENERY.

Scene I.—Local street scene in 2d grooves.

Scene II.—Kitchen—full set. Practicable staircase in the rear. Arched entrance
R. U. E. Practicable steps leading up to door L. Door R.

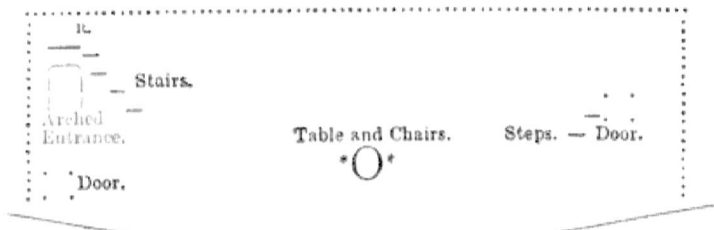

Scene III.—Handsome drawing-room in 2d grooves.

Scene IV.—Full set. Distant view of Washington from old State Fort. Doors,
R. U. E., R. and L. Set row in 3d grooves, representing ramparts of the fort; view of
Potomac by moonlight beyond.

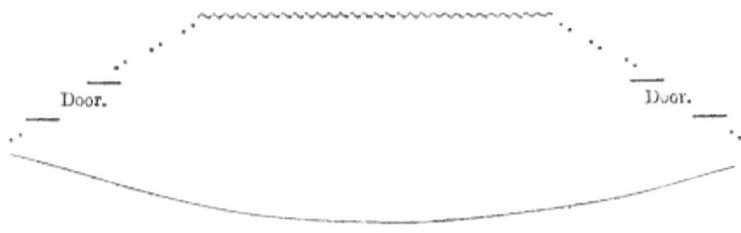

COSTUMES.

(*Of some Century or other ; it may be the eighteenth, with a Centennial flavor.*)

Count de Ferny.—Square-cut court coat, velvet, gold lace ; knee breeches, satin ;
silk stockings, and shoes and buckles ; powder or wig ; sword. (Cloak in last
scene for the escape.)

Bestfille.—Same as above, various coloring to suit.

Morris-and-Essex.—Knee breeches, satin ; silk stockings ; and upper portion of
costume and head to resemble Kelso, Chief of Police.

Piermi Shell.—Square-cut mulberry-colored coat, long and ragged, with a vest,
square-cut, variegated figured, cotton old flannel bed curtain chintz, and old
moleskin knee breeches ; gray homespun stockings ; short English gaiters up to
middle of calf ; slouched hat ; long iron-gray hair, bald on top. Make up cadav-
erous face.

Mule-in-Hay.—Full trunks, red ; brown square jacket ; shirt rough ; blonde wig ;
slouched hat. Make up white face, red nose. to represent a cold in the head.

Andrew—Square-cut plain cloth coat ; knee breeches, with stockings ; three cor-
nered hat.

Baroness.—Black velvet train dress, and bag wig.

Rosemi Shell—Neat brown French peasant dress, trimmed with black velvet ;
high black velvet peasant cap, trimmed with brown ; red stockings ; shoes and
buckles ; white fishen à la Marie Antoinette.

Susie.—Modern school-girl pinafore and short dress ; hair crimped and hanging
down back.

Suppers—French Gens d'Arms, with high grotesque hats.

PROPERTIES.

Swords; prayer-book; letters; pawn-check, and lottery ticket; huge bag of gold; large dog tied to rope; cards; glasses for drinks, and waiter; poison-powder; daggers; lump of glue.

SYNOPSIS, AND AUTHOR'S PREFACE.

This play claims to be a travesty of the melo-drama, "Rose Michel," as produced at the Union Square Theatre, New York, during the season of 1875–'76. As there presented it is the joint work of Messrs. Ernest Blum, and James Steele Mackaye. To the latter gentleman is due the credit of having eliminated all that was repulsive in the situations of the original French play. In this burlesque, the plot of the Mackaye-Blum drama is indicated in the absurdly strong light that travesty demands. The mother's extreme love of and devotion to her daughter, gives this parody its second title, "My Daughter! Oh, my Daughter!" The author has attempted, in the brief space allotted him by the theatre for which his work was written, to make his text as pointed and amusing as was consistent with the main idea of the plot. The very favorable manner in which "ROSEMI SHELL" was received by the manager, and the ladies and gentlemen of his company, leads the author to hope that his lines in printed form may meet with a fair share of the reader's appreciation. No songs have been introduced the words of which do not form a portion of the text; consequently, those that *are* here published have been copyrighted with the rest of the play. The characters of "ROSEMI SHELL" are of almost equal importance. The scenery is local, and is here given as arranged at Mr. Josh Hart's beautiful theatre, "The Eagle," under the artistic supervision of Matt Morgan. The author begs leave to return thanks to the management for the generous manner in which his play was placed on the boards.   S. R.

TIME IN REPRESENTATION—FIFTY MINUTES.

STAGE DIRECTIONS.

R. means Right of Stage, facing the Audience; L. Left; C. Centre; R. C. Right of Centre; L. C. Left of Centre. D. F. Door in the Flat, or Scene running across the back of the Stage; C. D. F. Centre Door in the Flat; R. D. F. Right Door in the Flat; L. D. F. Left Door in the Flat; R. D. Right Door; L. D. Left Door; 1 E. First Entrance; 2 E. Second Entrance; U. E. Upper Entrance; 1, 2 or 3 G. First, Second or Third Grooves.

R.   R. C.   C.   L. C.   L.

☞ The reader is supposed to be upon the stage facing the audience.

ROSEMI SHELL;

OR,

MY DAUGHTER! OH! MY DAUGHTER.

SCENE I.—*Street Scene (somewhere on the globe.)*

Enter BARON DE BESTFILLE. *He comes tripping jauntily down, and speaks most of his lines in a flippant, burlesque manner.*

BESTFILLE. Aha! oho! likewise ahem! In yonder
    There dwells the one I love, of whom I'm fonder
    Than of the world and all. Would I could do some
    Bold act to win her back wife of my bosom.
    Wife, did I say? Alas! I must repel her,
    For though she's mine, she's got another feller!
    She loves me not because I love too many.
    What folly that is! why, I'd love not any
    Unless I loved as many as I sought for.
    I'll love all that my money can be bought for.
    But soft! methinks I heard a gentle voice.
    Perhaps 'tis she—my own, my heart's own choice.
    (*looks off,* R.) Can she have left her house, me in the lurch?
    By Jove! I see her coming out of church.
    I'll seek an *honest* place where I can hide,
    Where, till the proper moment comes, I'll bide.
    (*to audience*) When I say hon-*nest* place to bide in,
    I've no allusion to the thought, nest-hidin'! (*he goes up stage to the side.*)

Enter BARONESS, L. U. E. (*slow music*). *She carries a prayer-book in front of her, and comes musingly down; speaks very impressively.*

BARONESS. Ah, from the mass I have this moment come,
    And pious words still in my ears do hum;
    Just let me think now what the preacher said;
    His thoughts were beautiful—oh, my poor head,
    I can't recall his words; yet, bliss of blisses,
    I'm sure he spoke of paroxysmal kisses,
    And ah! the smile that beamed upon his face
    When he discussed the thought, "another's place."
    I do not quite remember how't began,
    But he said something 'bout a better man.

BESTFILLE *hurries from his hiding-place down to her.* *She starts.*

BEST. (*in extr regant violence*). What! dare you tell me, woman, to
　　my face
　　That there's a better in your husband's place?
BAR. Eh? (*bewildered*) Who are you, strange man! begone, and hush.
　　You naughty thing, you really make me blush!
BEST. Begone? I'll not, nor any other be,
　　Until you come and go along with me!
BAR. With you!
BEST.　　　　　Yes, and at once obey;
　　For I'm your husband; mind now what you say.
BAR. My husband! mercy, can such things exist?
BEST. They can and do. (*he clutches her hand.*)
BAR.　　　　　Oh, stop; you'll hurt my wrist.
BEST. Come! I'll *wrist-store* you to your huggie's arms.
　　Come on, sweet creature; hush your wild alarms.
BAR. I won't.
BEST.　　　You must!
BAR.　　　　　　　I won't, I say!
BEST. But I say yes, so come.

Enter, boisterously, FERNY *from palace,* R. *He dashes wildly down, spreads
　　out his arms, draws sword, and cries*

FERNY (*burlesque melodrama*). Stay! villain! stay!
BEST. (*releasing her.* Who bids me stay? I'll not—my blood is riz!
BAR. (*in* FERNY's *arms*). Is it my darling?
FERN. (*to her*).　　　　　Of course it is.
BEST. Did you say *corset?* ah, that's good for you.
　　When you say *stay,* why, that's a *corset* too!
FERN. I have no time for idle *jest jest* now.
BEST. Then get you gone, and give me back my frow.
FERN. What do I hear? Speak, woman—ART HIS WIFE?
BAR. I art; but I love thee.
BEST. (*drawing sword*).　　I'll have thy life.
FERN. You will? Not much, I guess. Lay on, old hoss,
　　And damned be he who first cries, "Let up, boss." (*they make
　　a few thrusts.*)

Enter MORRIS-AND-ESSEX, R. U. E.

MORRIS (*up the stage, calls out*). Put up your arms! (*coming down*) Aye,
　　and your elbows too.
FERN. (*to* BESTFILLE). Say, stag his nibs.
BEST. (*to* MORRIS).　　　　Old Squeezix, who are you?
MORRIS. I'm prefect of the Seine. I'll have no chin;
　　Do as I bid you, or I'll run you in.
BEST. What were those words? It sounded very plain,
　　As though he said, "I'm perfectly insane."
FERN. (*to* MORRIS). I'll tell you, prefect, what the trouble is.
　　This lady here is——
BEST. (*interrupting.*)　　　　Mine!
MORRIS.　　　　　　　　Yours?
FERN. (*jealously*).　　　　　　　His?
MORRIS (*to* BARONESS). Whose wife, good woman, are you anyway?
BEST. Say mine.

Bar.   No longer.
Morris. (*pointing to* Ferny). His ?
Bar. (*coyly*).   I hope—some day.
Morris. Explain yourself, and stop th' immoral scene,
    And say in Anglo-Saxon whose you mean.
Bar. Well, then, I am—but no, that's not the thing.
    I cannot speak it; won't you let me sing !

SONG.—" Virtuous Though Free "

To the air of " Pas Ca," Madame L'Archiduc.

Oh,.folldi-roldi-lorri!! oh, don't think me immoral,
    Although you have a quarrel to learn whose wife I be ;
The secret of this bother, I'm neither one nor t'other,
Nor sister, wife, nor mother,
    For Love they say is free.
But ah, you can't, with all your quarrel,
Prove in court that I'm immoral ;
    For this much I can say flat,
No protection have I needed,
For no man has yet succeeded
    Even in obtaining *that*. (*bites her thumb and coquettes with audience.*)
Chorus.—Not that ! not that ! etc. (*repeat, with thumb business.*)
                    [Omnes *repeat chorus, and exeunt.*

SCENE II.-- *Kitchen in* Piermi's *house.*

Enter Piermi—*he comes down stealthily to the footlights, then draws him-
    self up, and speaks in tragic tones, with mock impressiveness.*

Piermi. My name is Piermi—but know all as well,
    I'm *shelldom* mentioned other than as *sheil !*
    Although my wife, the madam, I despise her,
    Says I am nothing but a *shelfish* miser.
    Shellfish ! Ha, ha ! I bet her silly prate
    Means that I am a little *lobster*-nate
    In paying over cash for dress and sham,
    I hate such idle show, 'taint worth a—straw ;
    But ah, my gold, my precious, precious gold, (*goes to trap-door,
        R. 2 E., and lifts out huge bag*)
    How many blessings have for thee been *sold !*
    How many men and women have for thee,
    Sweet precious darling, gold, been *sold* by me ?
    I've *sold* them all for *thee*, thou glittering gold,
    But thou my *soul*, for all this hast *consoled !* (*he hugs and kisses
        the bag in extravagant rapture*)
    Thou feast for peasant, prince, and all the nation.
    Hard money, *hard* to get ! curse to *inflation*. (Mule-in-Hay
        heard sneezing and coughing, without)
    But some one comes, sweet life and love, away ! (*bag disappears*)

Enter Mule-in-Hay ; *sneezes.*

Well, what do you want, you sneezing Mule-in-Hay ?

Mule's *nose is red, he wears a flanne' rag tied around his neck, and bears
    sundry other marks of a cold. He speaks through his nose, sounding
    b for m, and d for n.*

MULE. Kind master—(*pshew*) now who'd you 'spose
　　　Has sent me here ? (*sneezes*) Wait till I blow by dose. (*blows
　　　his nos: to music.*)
PIE :. Speak, speak ! who sent you here, was it your Missis ? (MULE
　　　shakes his head)
　　　Not ? Then my daughter, (MULE *shakes his head*) or her lover ?
　　　(MULE *shakes* This is
　　　Getting monotonous ; damn it, boy, speak !
MULE. Wait till I stop by dose ; it's got a leak. (*bus'ness.*)
PIER Tell me, you scoundrel—hear me—tell me, *who*, sir ?
MULE. P'ease, sir it was—ah some—(*sneeze*) some foreign snoozer.
PIER. (*aside*). A foreigner ! who can it be ?, No doubt
　　　He brings me gold, I'll have the secret out !
　　　(*aloud, to* MULE) Go tell him come, at once, I'll 'wait him here ;
　　　Bid welcome to the new come *foreigneer !*
MULE A *far an' near !* much better *far* than *near.*
　　　What business has a foreign snoozer here ?
　　　Ha ! let a snoozer in ?　No, not for Mike,
　　　He's got a look about him I don't like ! (*sneezes violently.*)
PIER. (*enraged*). You wretched sneezer ! what is that to you, sir ?
MULE. (*half aside*). I'd rather be a sneezer than a snoozer !
PIER Don't dare to argue, you catarrhal wretch,
　　　But dang it, go, the foreigner to fetch !
　　　　　　　　　　[*Hastens him off*, C , *then exits*, L.

　　　　　Enter ANDREW, *leading on* SUSIE.

ANDREW. Come on, sweet Susie, darling, laugh and cheer up,
　　　Be always *Susan*, love, my *Susan*-syrup.
SUSIE. Yes, darling, well I know what I should be ;
　　　But oh, my love, I'm thinking sad of thee.
AND. Sad, darling, sad ?　Oh, no, that must not be.
SUSIE. Well, listen, then, my dear, and you shall see,
　　　My precious Andy. Pandy. Handy, Andy,
　　　My sweet, delicious stick of sugar candy,
　　　How oft you've praised my face, and, with caresses,
　　　Admired all this hair that you called tresses ;
　　　But, darling, 'tis the thought of my back hair
　　　That fills my soul with grief, my mind with care,
　　　For, tell me, will you think me still as fair
　　　When this *here hair* will be no longer *there ;*
　　　In fact, when I have lost these locks, so called,
　　　Say, " will you love me, darling, when I'm bald ? "

　　　　　　　　　　SONG.

　　　AIR.—" *Will You Love Me when I'm Old ?* "

　　　　　I would ask of you, my darling,
　　　　　　A question soft and low,
　　　　　That gives me many a heart-ache,
　　　　　　As the moments come and go ;
　　　　　I know that now you love me
　　　　　　With a love that's passion called ;
　　　　　But this is what I would ask you,
　　　　　　Will you love me when I'm bald ?
　　　　　But this is what I would ask you,
　　　　　　Will you love me when I'm bald ?

CHORUS.

We'll soon be gone forever,
  Unto other regions called ;
But my heart will know no sadness
  If you'll love me when I'm bald.

ANDREW. Darling, do not ask conundrums,
  I've told you oft before
Your getting bald will only make
  Love like mine grow more and more ;
Though each single hair be missing,
  By your head my heart's enthralled,
Though you have to wear a wig, dear,
  I will love you when you're bald.
Though you have to wear a wig, dear,
  I will love you when you're bald.

CHORUS.

We'll soon be gone forever,
  Unto other regions called ;
But your heart will know no sadness,
  For I'll love you when you're bald.

[*They walk off,* R.

Enter BESTFILLE, *followed by* MULE, *who drags on a monstrous bull-dog, tied to a rope.*

BEST. Where is the lovely maid ? Send her to me, sir !
MULE. I'll see you blowed first. (*sneeze*) Here catch him, Cæsar !
BEST. Then send her father here that I may court her
  With gold——

Enter, wildly, ROSEMI. *Music.*

ROSE. (*tragic attitude*), My daughter ! oh, my daughter !
BEST. Halloa ! She's got them bad ; there's something wrong.
  (*to* MULE) Clear out, you wretch, and take that dog along.
  (*pushing*) Go, hurry, lazy bones ! go, travel faster !
  And quickly hither send your Mister Master !
ROSE. (*wildly*). Where is the one I love ; oh, who has caught her !
  O, give me back my daughter ! Oh, my daughter !
MULE. (*tying rope of dog to table-leg*). I'll leave this bull-pup here till I
  come back.
  (*to dog*) If he behaves not *well*, just *sick* him, Jack !   [*Exit.*
ROSE. (*still wildly*). And have you, villain, hither come and sought 'er ?
  My daughter, darling, darling ; oh, my daughter !
BEST. (*aside*). She acts as though the roof were falling on her,
  I really think there's something crawling on her !

Enter PIERMI.

Ha ! glad to see thee, Piermi ! know the news ?
To win a fortune, would'st thy daughter lose,
And let her be my wife——
PIER.   Hush ! not so loud—
  Th' old woman's watching ! Ro emi, "blease go oud."

ROSE. (*strikes attitude*). Base wretches, both, with shame you quiver
oughter!
And would you sell my daughter? Oh, my daughter!

BEST. No, Madam—sell the damsel? No! be cal,m!

PIER. (*aside*). Egad! I had much rather sell the *dam*!
But dams they say as well as *damsels* old,
Are, so experience shows, *dam sel dom sold*!

BEST. Well, sir!

PIER. Wife Rosemi! leave the room at once,
And don't be dancing round here like a dunce. (*push ng her
up to* L. D.)

ROSE O, let me throw myself into the water!
For they would steal my daughter! O, my daughter! [*Exits.*

PIER. (*moves table and chairs*, c., *sees dog*). Why, thunderin' lightning!
what confounded noodle
Has hitched this table-leg to that 'ere poodle?

*Loosens the rope—exit dog. They are about to seat themselves at table—
ROSEMI sticks her head out through the door, and sings to the chorus
of "Pull down the Blind."*

SONG.

Don't think I'm blind, don't think I'm blind!
Oh, I am not at all one of that kind;
Though you are left behind, bear this in mind,
Some one is looking! oh, don't think I'm blind!

(*speaks*) "My daughter! oh, my daughter!" (*disappears.*)

PIER. (*hurries to the door and locks it. They seat themselves.* PIERMI
draws out a pack of cards. Storm is heard i di tance. Let's
have a game.

BEST. All right, begin——

PIER. (*shuffling cards*). But say——

BEST. How much do you want for her?

PIER. How much'll you pay?

BEST. I'll give you sixty thousand down in cash!

PIER. (Your deal)! No, no, my boy; the thing won't wash!
No, no; indeed! I tell you flat, I shan't!

BEST. Then dang, it fellow, how much do you want?

PIER. (*after a pause—he shuffles the cards*) One hundred thousand—
(*pause*)—here, cut!

BEST. (*jumping up,* L. C., *in amazement*). Shell! Shell! Shell! You're off
your nut!

PIER. Sneezer! (*calling off* R., *then to* BESTFILLE). What do you want
to drink?

BEST. Gin cock-tail with some lemon-peel I think—
Won't you take less——

PIER. No; talking is no use!
Sneezer, one cock-tail, and one Santa Cruz!
Just go to bed, and think the matter over;
The girl is cheap, if you do really love her. (*they rise*)
You look fatigued, and are so, I presume;
I'll have your cock-tail brought up to your room!
So go to bed now, think about the price;
I know you will say yes—take my advice

BEST. (*going up steps, off* L.). I'll think the matter over, and I guess
To-morrow I shall give my answer, 'yes." [*Exits.*

PIER. To-morrow! ah, methinks my plan's the way

Whereby your morrow will be yesterday,
And you will wish your "yes" had answered been,
Before the *yes*-terday you'd ever seen!

Enter SNEEZER, *with drinks.*

Give me the cock-tail. (*pouring in a powder to lightning*) Put
   more sugar in—
'Twill give a better flavor to the gin.
     [SNEEZER *takes gin into room, returns, and exits.*
PIER. (*takes his drink, then goes to the table and takes out two big butcher*
   knives). Come, potent daggers, to your wealthy plunder,
And help me, instruments of blood and thunder! (*music, and*
   thunder.)

ROSEMI *enters, as he creeps towards door, through secret entrance She fol-*
lows his steps in burlesque imitation, and watches him go into room—
then sings.

SONG.—DON'T THINK I'M BLIND.

Re-enter PIERMI; *starts as he sees* ROSEMI. *He holds the red knives aloft,*
then drops them.

ROSE. What have you done? O! wretch, I *saw* you!
PIER. (*fiercely*). Be silent, woman, or by Jove I'll claw you! (*sings.*)

SONG.

AIR.—"*Stolen Kisses from Girofle!*"

What do I care for your spying,
   For your chin or for your jaw?
Though there can be no denying
   Of the bloody deed you saw?

What do *I* care for your spying,
   What care I for what you saw—
For your prying, or your lying,
   For your chin or for your jaw?

(*speaks tragically*) Because I dare you, woman, though you
   chose,
I dare you, double dare you, to expose!

Enter SUSIE *and* ANDREW.

For there is one who loves me, *you* have taught her,
Behold her there! (*pointing to* SUSIE.)
ROSE. (*rushing wildly into her arms*). My daughter! Oh, my daughter!

Enter MULE—*sneezes.*

MULE. Where is my missis? Every where I've sought her!
ROSE. Oh, oh! my daughter, darling! oh, my daughter!
PIER. (*grindingly*). Her daughter! she oughter have taught 'er in-
   stead of to prize me
    To sorter, well—oughter—have taught 'er perhaps to despise
    me!

All sing Chorus.

> What does he care for our spying—
> What does he care what we saw?
> For our prying, or our lying,
> For our chin, or for our jaw?

Repeat, then they all dance. Finally, SUSIE *tumbles into* ROSEMI'S *arms,
who cries:* " My daughter! O, my daughter!' *Scene closes in.*

SCENE III.—*Chamber in the De Ferny Palace,* **handsomely** *painted flat.
Writing-table* **to be** *carried* **on.** *Large doors in* C.

Enter MORRIS and FERNY.

FERN. What horrid news, say you has been transmitted?
 A *rank* offence in our *ranks* committed!
MOR. Ay, and a nobleman the victim is!
 The Baron Bestfille—oh, how sad it is!
FERN. 'Tis sad, but still I've heard great many moot
 That he was nothing but an old galloot.
MOR. Young man, beware, you know not what you say,
 If a policeman heard you, you would have to pay
 Most dearly for these words—for so detected
 You will as criminal be first suspected.
 So, mind your eye—I must from hence be getting,
 To buy my chances in a pool-room betting! [*Exit,* R.
FERN. I'll to the Baroness's chamber haste,
 She is a widow now; no time to waste! [*Exit.*

Enter ROSEMI, C.

ROSE. Oh, ma. oh, may! oh, me! oh, my! oh, mo!
 I am the worst used of ge-*nus* homo!
 Oh, mo! oh, ma! oh, may! oh, me! oh, my!
 I am so sad I really want to cry!
 That act of Shell's so bad, I'd like t'have *hissed him!*
 But oh! that isn't down in Delsarte's system.
 Upon the victim's body there were found
 These papers here—Shell dropped them on the ground.
 I picked them up—I've brought them here! I know
 They are the Count's, his name is on them; oh,
 Is it for this my husband dealt in gore?
 A pawn-check—four-eleven-forty-four!
 Oh, mercy on us! can't one's life be hid?
 To think for *this,* my Shell has murder *did!*
 It grieves me *sore* to know for *sor-did* greed,
 That is no *sort* o' gain, he *sort* that deed!
 I'll bring these treasures to their first head-quarter;
 Then give me back my daughter! Oh, my daughter!
  [*Places the papers in table-drawer, and exits,* R.

Enter, hurriedly, MORRIS, L., *holding* FERNY *by the throat.*

MOR. Deceitful wretch! Assassin! is it true,
 The Count Bestfille has emptied been by you?
FERN. Unhand me! What! Great rocks! A murderer, I?
 Great thundering Keeley motor, it's a lie!

Mor. Ah, but the *proof*, 'gainst which you are not *proof*,
　　The evidence of crime's beneath this roof!
Fern. Where, liar, where! Show me!
Mor. 　　　　　　　　　　　　This way!
　　Pawn-ticket! that's the first, next, so they say,
　　Four-eleven-forty-four—these things were stole,
　　And you possess them, Shell has told the whole! (*goes to table
　　　　and takes them out*)
　　Ah, Shell spoke true! Here, villain; son of Adam!
Fern. (*aside, baffled*). By gum, they're *there!* I thought old Bestfille
　　had 'em!
Mor. Your doom is sealed; to prison you must go,
　　There to be sentenced. Guards without there, ho!

Enter Guards.

　　Here, seize the villain! for the crime is his'n,
　　And to the Tombs straightway take him to prison. (Guards
　　　seize him)
　　Don't stop to argue, 'tis no use; away! (*turns aside. Music.*)

Enter, wildly, Rosemi.

Rose. Stay—stay—stay! (*tragic flourish*) Stay! (*gasping for breath*)
　　The world all lies! my blood at last has risen!
　　You're cartin' off a guiltless man to prison—
　　He did not do the deed! The crime's not his'n!
　　Another did the deed! one old and wizen.
　　Don't hang the young man, oh! the crime's not his'n!
　　Don't, by mis*take*, the young man *take* to prison!
Fern. O, save me! tell them *who* the murd'rer is!

Enter Piermi, c.

Pier. Don't be so fresh, young man, just mind your biz.
Rose. (*tragical*). At sight of him, great lands, my brain grows wild!
　　Behold the——
Pier. (*silencing her with a gesture*). Cheese it! (*speaking off*) Come in
　　here, my child. (*Music. Leads on* Susie, *followed by* An-
　　drew.)
　　Here is our Susie, and her young escorter!
Rose. (*very wildly*). Oh, oh, oh, oh! my daughter! Oh, my daughter!

Enter Mule, *dragging on dog;* Rosemi *falls quivering and gasping at* Susie's
feet.

Mor. Away to prison, the crime is his'n!
　　The crime is his'n, away to prison! (*the* Guards *lead him off—
　　repeating to music several times*)
Omnes. Away to prison, the crime is his'n;
　　The crime is his'n, away to prison!

Positions.

Rosemi, c., *on floor.*

R.	R. C.	L. C.	L.
Piermi.	Susie (*kneeling*).	Andrew.	Mule.
Morris.			Dog.

Piermi *dances about* Rosemi's *body,* singing.

SONG.

What do I care for your spying, etc. (MORRIS *and* MULE *join in*.)

CHORUS.—What does he care, etc.

ROSEMI *revires, is raised by* SUSIE *and* ANDREW, *bewildered for a moment; as she is being led off,* L. *recovers in a fit of rapture, and exclaims, hugging* SUSIE: "*My daughter! oh, my daughter!*" *Exits, with* ANDREW *and* SUSIE. *The others follow, with* PIERMI *and* MORRIS, *arm-in-arm, dancing to the tune and words of chorus. Exit* MORRIS *and* PIERMI; *then exit* MULE (*with* DOG), *also dancing and singing. He sneezes as he goes off.*

SCENE LAST.—*Ramparts of the old State Fort, with a distant view of Washington on the Potomac by moonlight.*

Enter SUSIE, *holding a letter.*

SUSIE. Unhappy me! My Andrew writes this letter,
    And asks what mamma has that does so fret her.
    He fears there's something awful on her mind,
    And if there is, and he the cause can find,
    And learns that over me there comes disgrace,
    He'll never come again before my face.
    Alas, I thought for naught my love could leave me,
    Alas, I never thought he'd so deceive me!
    (*spoken very sadly*) Ah, when I think of all the things he's said
    That were so nice, my eyes grow moist, in bed,
    And I recall with burning tears that scald,
    His promise still to love me when I'm bald. [*Exit, mournfully.*

Enter PIERMI—*he sings to the air of "The Scamp."*

SONG.

THE DARN'DEST OF SCAMPS.

I flatter myself I'm a scamp,
    A double-dyed villain, egad!
A scally-wag, rascal, and rogue,
    And everything else that is bad;
I proved to my parents a bane,
    A perfect young fiend to my nurse,
And every year that I spend on this sphere,
    I am getting from bad to worse.

CHORUS.

If ever there was an old scamp,
    I flatter myself I am he;
From William the Norman, to Brigham the Mormon,
    They can't hold a candle to me.

When first I began to cavort,
    A tiny young shaver of six;
The first thing I did of a villainous sort
    Was to smash all our kittens with bricks;

Just one year from then an old hen
  I captured, my age was but seven,
I got a sky-rocket hitched on to her socket,
  And sent the old chicken to heaven.

CHORUS.

If ever, there was an old scamp,
  I flatter myself I am he ;
From a Sunday-school teacher, to Henry Ward Beecher,
  They can't hold a candle to me.

At twelve I was boss of the town,
  Had mashed every kid there was 'nigh ;
Laid every lad low, with a fearful knock down,
  And given each one a black-eye ;
At twenty I worked in the banks.
  And was known as a deuce of a salter ;
One day—as they say—I broke loose from the ranks,
  And the papers all called me " defaulter."

CHORUS

If ever there was an old scamp,
  I flatter myself I am he ;
From a free-loving Mormon, to Duncan and Sherman,
  They can't hold a candle to me.

I have sworn, I have burglared, and stolen,
  I have chiselled and blackmailed, and lied ;
In fact, I don't know of a crime every time,
  That I couldn't commit if I tried !
I flatter myself I'm a scamp,
  A deuced immense one, egad !
A doubled-dyed villain, and rascal, and rogue,
  And everything else that is bad.

CHORUS.

If ever there was an old scamp,
  I flatter myself I am he ;
From to the head of the Nixes, to the Boss of Big Sixes,
  They can't hold a candle to me.

PIER. (*speaks*). My wife and Morris have a plan *on foot*,
  And want me here *on hand* to help them do't !
They want to set that Count de Ferny free.
Great Moses ! what will then become of me ?
If I help *him*, then to the wall *I'm* jammed ;
Not much, I guess. Ha ! if I do, I'm damned !
With Rosemi I shall have a *tiff, that's plain*—
She's trying on her *plain-tiff* dodge again ;
I'll carry warning to the sup'rintendent,
And close the *carry-'ere* of the defendant.   [*Exit*. R.

Enter MULE-IN-HAY, *with* DOG.

MULE (*very sadly*). I bring unto the Count this terrier here,
  The last sad offering on this earthly sphere.
My Pollywog ain't pretty, but he's good,
I've trained him proper, as a parent should ;

When he feels in the *mood* he can say " Thankee !"
Can *hold the fort* like *Moody and like Sankey !*
Besides I've trained him to perform some tricks,
To chew shoe-leather and to swallow sticks,
And, what is harder still—he's often done't—
I've taught him how to wag his tail in front.
His nose is moist, like mine, his eyes are grayish,
He has a youthful Blum, quite Steele-Mackayish.
To thee. De Ferny, I this purp do send
On *purpose* to convince thee I'm thy friend.
I'd like to give him (*sneeze*) in a speech well said,
But, oh, this horrid cold here in my head ! (*sneeze*.)

Sings, to the air of " Hilderbrand Montrose," the following original Sneezing-
Song.

SNEEZING SONG.

Copyrighted by SYDNEY ROSENFELD.

I have a constant ailing dose,
     In vain I try to stop it ;
I've used all ointments hot, and froze,
     To plaster and to prop it ;
Sometimes I do dot bind it,
     But when to speak I care,
And find I can't get started,
     It albost bakes be swear !

CHORUS.

P'shew*—p'shew !*   Oh, by poor dose !
By throat is hot as blazes, but the other parts are froze ;
I'd like to tell a story of my troubles and my woes,
But oh, I cannot do it—there's a stoppage id by doze !

Exit MULE, *but returns to meet* MORRIS, *who enters.*

MOR.   Ah, Mule-in-Hay, go set that bull-dog free,
     And tell your Mrs. straight to come to me.
MULE (*in a shrill voice*). I fly, my Lord ! I fly ! (*hands off the dog.*)
MOR.   But stop, come back !
     (*giving him lump of glue*) Take this cement ; your voice has got
         a crack,
     Just take that crack and have it close *cemented !*
MULE. He looks so serious, *you'd s'pose he meant it !*
     A *crack* at me intended, it's a fact !
     But if this thing can fix a voice that's cracked,
     How would it do for me to send a bit
     To what's-his-name ? his has got a split !
MOR.   Your own is just as bad, you needn't taunt.
MULE. But *he* can keep it up ; you know *I* can't.
MOR.   Keep *up* a voice so high ! I'd keep it *down.*
MULE. Oh, that's *Stuart* on Robson ; I'd leave town
     If my voice lasted so perennial,
     Or else I'd box it up for the Centennial.   [*Exits*, L.
MOR. (*calling off*). Turnkey, send out your prisoner to me.

                     * Sneeze !

Enter FERNY.

FERNY. Morris-and-Essex, can't you set me free?
    I am not guilty; why then must I suffer?
    I am the victim of some other duffer.
    Can you not find some plea?—I hate profanity—
    But damn it, man, can't you make out "*insanity?*"
MOR. Won't wash—been tried too many times before,
    Although perhaps in your case 'tmight help more,
    Because the judge and jury would not doubt you,
    You always have a crazy look about you.
FERN. Don't *guy* me, please, for I your *guidance* need.
    Pray let me slip, and make believe I'm Tweed.
MOR. No; hold your oars and roars, I'll free you still,
    Although 'tis death to help a man who'd kill.
    Go, wait in there until the signal's guv,
    And know I yield my duty to my love!
FERN. Good 'nough, old man, I'll bet my boots on you!
    But tell me what and where you'll signal to.
MOR. On yonder lower side, for that best suits.
    Await the cry of "Rumpty foozle snoots." [*Hurries him off.*
    I'll go now for a drop of soda water,
    And then I'll——

Enter ROSEMI.

ROSE.   Oh, my daughter! oh, my daughter!
    Oh, Morris, and oh, Essex, and owe all!
    Oh, Crucible, and oh, *A. Oakey Hall!*
    My husband, yielding to my prayers and hopes,
    Has promised to come here with lots of ropes,
    To help us—not to hang by, though he oughter;
    (*aside*) But hush—I nearly had betrayed my daughter.
MOR. Here is the trap-door down which he must go.
    (*after hunting for a trap-door*) I've managed *stages* long enough
        to know
    Where trap-doors are, in fact, I have gone through 'em
    E'en since those far back days of JOHNNY BROUGHAM.
ROSE. The time draws nigh for Piermi Shell to come!
    O Piermi! Piermi! (*pause*) All is still and dumb.

PIERMI *is seen looking over back wall and pointing out spot to a* GUARD.
ROSEMI *and* MORRIS *walk off in different directions very quietly.*

PIER. (*sings*). Don't think I'm blind! (*disappears.*)

Re-enter ROSEMI. *Sings to the waltz song of Girofle.*

ROSE.   O Piermi Shell,
         Where are you, tell?
    Why don't you come where you "had oughter"?
         For don't you know,
         If you don't, oh,
    What will become of our beautiful daughter?

Re-enter PIERMI.

At last, at last! He's come at last, at last!

Re-enter MORRIS.

MOR. At last, at last! He's come, he's come at last, at last!

Re-enter MULE.

MULE. At last! at last! at last! at last! at last!

ROSE ⎰
MOR. ⎱ At last we seize you, and we *sees you* last.

PIER. You see *shoe-last!* O, no! you do not do't!
I'm not a *last*, nor slipper, shoe nor boot. (MORRIS *beckons—
they go about mysteriously, looking for the trap-door, singing to
the "Conspirators' Chorus."*)

CONSPIRATORS' CHORUS.

Madame Angot.

We'll find the place before we go,
We'll find the place before we go,
And then we'll dive way down below!
And then we'll dive way down below!
But give the sign, oh give the sign
That shall define our meaning fine.

Oh, umpty foozle-oozle—oh, shnoots!
Oh, rumpty foozle-oozle—shoots!
Oh, rump-ty—f-o-o-o-o-o-zle—shnoots!

Enter FERNY—*joins in.*

Oh, rumpty foozle-oozle—shnoots!
Oh, rumpty foozle-oozle—shnoots!
Oh, rumpty—fo-o-o-o-o-zle—shnoots!

*They join hands and walk around the trap-door in a circle. Enter, from
opposite entrances, facing each other,* ANDREW *and* SUSAN, *dressed as
the Light Shell Guard. They sing.*

SONG.

AIR.—"*Skidmore Guard.*"

We've made it up, we're friends again, are Andy and his Sue;
We love each dearer now than ever, and more true!
Though Pa and Ma may have a row, or get into a fight,
We young ones never shall get mad, because it isn't right.

March around and kiss.

Deary, deary,
Come right herey!
Kiss me, cheery
Once or twice;
That's right, honey,
It's awful funny,
But it's ever so nice!

After song they march to music, up c., *and remain locked in each other's arms.
The others come down, after having been walking round the trap-door, and*

then spread and right about. FERNY *is led by* MORRIS *to the trap-door ; but just as he raises it, cries are heard without, and* PIERMI, L. 1 E., *claps his hands and shouts.*

ROSE. (R. 1 E.). Oh, mercy on us all! We are betrayed ; (*she sees picture of lovers embraced.*)

     Enter GUARDS—*they seize* FERNY, *and take him* R.

Oh, no! not him! At last my debt is paid,
She's happy now; her love has blessing brought her.
Then let me speak, my daughter, oh, my daughter!
That man is not the man—your man crawls there!
A wretched murderer, a rascal rare.

All fall back and look at PIERMI, *crouched at* R. U. E. (*he having sneaked round there during* ROSEMI'S *speech.*) *He draws himself up, and then makes a run for opposite entrance.*

MOR. Aim, fire! aim, fire! Aim higher! and fire higher!
Aim, fire! aim higher! fire higher! higher fire!

GUARDS *have fired.* PIERMI *falls,* C., *over trap-door ; all but* GUARDS *dance around him, singing to the previous air of* " *Stolen Kisses from Girofle.* "

OMNES.   He is dead! oh, he is dead!
And it serves him right-ight-ight!
He at last has found his bed,
So good night! good night! good night!

They repeat ; at the finish of second verse, PIERMI *jumps up and sings :*

What do I care for your lying,
What care I for what you saw?
For your—(*about to dance.*)

GUARD *hurries down from back, and hits him over the head with stuffed rifle-butt. He falls flat, and dies.* OMNES *pointing to picture of* SUSIE *in* ROSEMI'S *arms, up* C.

CHORUS.

AIR.—" *Madame Angot.* "

She's the daughter—she's the daughter!
She's the daughter of Rosemi Shell ;
She's the daughter, darling daughter,
She's the daughter of Rosemi Shell! (*Repeat.*)

Lime light and Curtain in Tableau.

"Sweetest Shakspere, Nature's child,
Warbles his native wood-notes wild."—MILTON.

☞ Please notice that nearly all the Comedies, Farces and Comediettas in the following List of "DE WITT'S ACTING PLAYS" are very suitable for representation in small Amateur Theatres and on Parlor Stages, as they need but little extrinsic aid from complicated scenery or expensive costumes. They have attained their deserved popularity by their droll situations, excellent plots, great humor and brilliant dialogues, no less than by the fact that they are the most perfect in every respect of any edition of Plays ever published either in the United States or Europe, whether as regards purity of the text, accuracy and fulness of stage directions and scenery, or elegance of typography and clearness of printing.

*** In ordering, please copy the figures at the commencement of each piece, which indicate the number of the piece in "DE WITT'S LIST OF ACTING PLAYS."

☞ Any of the following Plays sent, postage free, on receipt of price—fifteen cents.

Address, **ROBERT M. DE WITT,**

No. 33 Rose Street, New York.

DE WITT'S ACTING PLAYS.

No.

1 CASTE. An original Comedy in three acts, by T. W. Robertson. A lively and effective satire upon the times, played successfully in America, at Wallack's. Five male and three female characters. Costumes, modern. Scenery, the first and third acts, interior of a neat room ; the second a fashionable room. Time in representation, two hours and forty minutes.

2 NOBODY'S CHILD. A romantic Drama in three acts, by Watts Phillips. Eighteen male and three female characters. A domestic drama, wonderfully successful in London, as it abounds in stirring scenes and capital situations. Costumes modern, suited to rural life in Wales. Scenery is wild and picturesque. Time in representation, two hours and a quarter.

3 £100,000. An original Comedy in three acts, by Henry J. Byron. Eight male and four female characters. A most effective piece, played with applause at Wallack's. Costumes of the day. Two scenes are required—a comfortably furnished parlor and an elegant apartment. Time in representation, one hour and three quarters.

DE WITT'S ACTING PLAYS.

41 BEAUTIFUL FOREVER. A Farce in one act, by Frederick Hay. Two male and two female characters. A sprightly satirical rebuke to those that patronize advertised nostrums. Costumes of the day. Scene, a handsome interior. Time in representation, forty minutes.

42 TIME AND THE HOUR. A Drama in three acts, by J. Palgrave Simpson and Felix Dale. Seven male and three female characters. An excellent acting play, full of life and incident, the parts of Medlicott and Marian Beck being capable of impressive representation—all others good. Costumes of the present period. Scenery, gardens and exterior, cottage and garden, **and** an old oaken chamber. Time in representation, two hours and a half.

43 SISTERLY SERVICE. An original Comedietta in **one** act, by J. P. Wooler. Seven male and two female characters. An interesting piece. Costumes, rich dresses of the musketeers of Louis XIII. Scenes, **an apartment of** that period, **and a corridor in the** royal palace of France. **Time** in representation, forty **minutes.**

44 WAR TO THE KNIFE. a Comedy in three acts, by Henry J. Byron. Five male and four female characters. A pleasing, entertaining and morally instructive lesson as to extravagant living; capitally adapted to the stage. Costumes of the present time. Scenes, three interiors. **Time** in representation, one hour and three quarters.

45 OUR DOMESTICS. A Comedy Farce in two acts, by Frederick Hay. Six male and six female characters. An irresistibly facetious exposition of high life below stairs, and of the way in which servants **treat** employers during their absence. Costumes of the day. Scenes, **kitchen and dining** room. Time in representation, one hour and a half.

46 MIRIAM'S CRIME. A Drama in three acts, by H. T. Craven. Five male and two female characters. One of the best acting plays, and easily put on the stage. Costumes modern. Scenery, modern English interiors, two in number. Time in representation, two hours.

47 EASY SHAVING. A Farce in one act, by F. C. Burnand and Montagu Williams. Five male and two female characters. A neat and effective piece, with excellent parts for low comedian and singing chamber maid. Costumes of the days of Charles II of England. Scene, a barber's shop. Time in representation, twenty-five minutes.

48 LITTLE ANNIE'S BIRTHDAY. An original personation Farce, by W. E. Suter. Two male **and four** female characters. A good farce, whose effectiveness depends upon a singing young lady, who could make the piece a sure success. Costumes modern. Scene, an apartment in an English country house. Time in representation, twenty-five minutes.

49 THE MIDNIGHT WATCH. A Drama in one act, by J. Maddison Morton. Eight male and two female characters. A successful little play. Costumes of the time of **the** French Revolution of 1795. **Scene,** the platform of a fortress. Time in representation, one hour.

50 THE PORTER'S KNOT. A serio-comic Drama in two acts, by John Oxenford. Eight male **and** two female characters. Interesting and thoroughly dramatic. Costumes of the day. Scenes, an interior of cottage and exterior of seaside hotel. Time in representation, one hour and **a quarter.**

51 A MODEL OF A WIFE. A Farce in one act, by Alfred Wigan. Three male and two female characters. Most amusing in conception and admirably carried out. Costumes of the day. Scene, a painter's studio. Time in representation, thirty-five minutes.

52 A CUP OF TEA. A Comedietta in one act. Translated from the French of *Une Tasse de Thé*, by Charles Nuttier and J. Derley. Three male and one female characters. An exquisite petty comedy, well adapted for amateur representation. Costumes modern. Scene, handsome drawing room. Time in representation, thirty minutes.

65 **CHECKMATE.** A Comedy in two acts, by Andrew Halliday. Six male and five female characters. Costumes, English, of the present day. Scenes, interior of a country hotel, and exterior of same, with landscape. Time in representation, one hour and a half.

66 **THE ORANGE GIRL.** A Drama in a prologue and three acts, by Harry Leslie and Nicholas Rowe. Eighteen male and four female characters. Costumes of the present day; this piece requires considerable scenery, and some of an especial nature. Time in representation, two hours and a quarter.

67 **THE BIRTHPLACE OF PODGERS.** A Farce in one act, by John Hollingshead. Seven male and three female characters. A capital acting extravaganza, introducing a number of eccentric personages. Costumes of the present time. Scene, a workingman's room. Time in representation, forty minutes.

68 **THE CHEVALIER DE ST. GEORGE.** A Drama in three acts, adapted from the French of MM. Velesville and Roger de Beauvoir, by T. W. Robertson. Nine male and three female characters. A very popular and favorite play. Costumes, very rich, in velvet, court and hunting dresses, breeches, stockings, &c. Scenery, a tavern and garden, an interior, style Louis Seize, and a plainer interior. Time in representation, one hour and a half.

69 **CAUGHT BY THE CUFF.** A Farce in one act, by Frederick Hay. **Four male and one** female characters. An exquisitely ludicrous production, crammed with situations. Costumes of the day. Scene, a kitchen. Time in representation, forty minutes.

70 **THE BONNIE FISHWIFE. A Farce in one act, by** Charles Selby, Comedian. Three male and one female characters. A very sprightly piece, in which the lady is required to sing, and to be capable of assuming the Scottish dialect. The costumes, although modern, involve eccentric Scottish and deer stalking dresses. Scenes, a handsome chamber and interior of Highland cottage. Time of playing, forty-five minutes.

71 **DOING FOR THE BEST.** A domestic Drama in two acts, by M. Rophino Lacy. Five male and three female characters. An effective acting piece, popular in London. Costumes of the day. Two scenes, one interior of cottage, the other a drawing room. Time in representation, one hour and a half.

72 **A LAME EXCUSE. A Farce in** one act, by **Frederick** Hay. Four male and two female characters. Costumes of the day. Scene, a handsome interior. Time in represention, thirty-five minutes.

73 **A GOLDEN FETTER (FETTERED).** A Drama in three acts, by Watts Phillips. Eleven male and four female characters. Costumes of the present time. Scenery extensive and peculiar to the piece. Time in representation, one hour and a half.

74 **THE GARRICK FEVER. A Farce in one act, by J. R.** Planche. Seven male and four female characters. Costumes of the year 1742—court dresses, regimentals, velvet trains, &c. Scenery, a plain interior. Time of representation, forty-five minutes.

75 **ADRIENNE; or, the Secret of a Life.** Drama in three acts, by Harry Leslie. Seven male and three female characters. A telling romantic drama. Italian and French costumes, civil and military. Scenery, elaborate interiors and landscapes. Time in representation, one hour and forty-five minutes.

76 **THE CHOPS OF THE CHANNEL. An original** Nautical Farce in one act, by Frederick Hay. Three male and two female characters. A very mirth exciting and whimsical composition. Costumes of the present day. Scene, the saloon of a steamer. Time in representation, forty minutes.

DE WITT'S ACTING PLAYS.

No.

158 SCHOOL. A Comedy in four acts, by T. W. Robertson. Six male and six female characters. Is a very superior piece, and has three characters unusually good for either sex. Could be played with fine effect at a girls' seminary. Costumes modern. Scenery, English landscape and genteel interiors. Time in representation, two hours and forty minutes.

159 IN THE WRONG HOUSE. A Farce in one act, by Martin Becher. Four male and two female characters. A very justly popular piece. Two of the male characters are excellent for light and low comedian. Good parts, too, for a young and old lady. Costumes modern. Scenery, an ordinary room. Time in representation, twenty-five minutes.

160 BLOW FOR BLOW. A Drama in a Prologue and three acts, by Henry J. Byron. Eleven male and six female characters. Full of homely pathos as well as rich humor. Has several excellent parts. Costumes modern. Scenery, interiors of offices and dwellings. Time in representation, three hours.

161 WOMAN'S VOWS AND MASONS' OATHS. In four acts, by A. J. H. Duganne. Ten male and four female characters. Has effective situations, fine characters and beautiful dialogues. Costumes modern, with Federal and Confederate uniforms. Scenery, interiors in country houses, and warlike encampments. Time in performance, two hours and thirty minutes.

162 UNCLE'S WILL. A Comedietta in one act, by S. Theyre Smith. Two male and one female characters. A brilliant piece; can be easily played in a parlor. Costumes modern, and naval uniform for Charles. Scenery, set interior drawing room. Time in representation, thirty minutes.

163 MARCORETTI. A romantic Drama in three acts, by John M. Kingdom. Ten male and three female characters. A thrillingly effective piece, full of strong scenes. Costumes, brigands and rich Italian's dress. Scenery, interior of castle, mountain passes, and princely ball room. Time in representation, two hours.

164 LITTLE RUBY; or, Home Jewels. A domestic Drama in three acts, by J. J. Wallace. Six male and six female characters. This drama is at once affecting and effective. Little Ruby fine personation for young prodigy. Costumes modern. Scenery, interior of dwelling and gardens. Time in representation, two hours.

165 THE LIVING STATUE. A Farce in one act, by Joseph J. Dilley and James Allen. Three male and two female characters. Brimful of fun. Trotter a great character for a droll low comedian. Costumes modern, with one old Roman warrior dress. Scenery, a plain interior.

166 BARDELL vs. PICKWICK. A Farcical sketch in one act, arranged from Charles Dickens. Six male and two female characters. Uncommonly funny. Affords good chance to 'take off'' local legal celebrities. Costumes modern. Scenery, a court room. Time in performance, thirty minutes.

167 APPLE BLOSSOMS. A Comedy in three acts, by James Albery. Seven male and three female characters. A pleasing piece, with rich part for an eccentric comedian. Costumes modern English. Scenery, exterior and interior of inn. Time in representation, two hours and twenty minutes.

168 TWEEDIE'S RIGHTS. A Comedy in two acts, by James Albery. Four male and two female characters. Has several excellent characters. John Tweedie, powerful personation; Tim Whiffler very funny. Costumes modern. Scenery, a stone mason's yard and modest interior. Time in representation, one hour and twenty-five minutes.

No.

181 and 182 QUEEN MARY. A Drama, by Alfred Tennyson. The only unmutilated edition. Arranged for the stage in four acts. [The portions of the play to be omitted in representation are very carefully marked.] Edited by John M. Kingdom. Thirty-seven male, nine female characters. A noble play, full of grand characters, and grave, sonorous and exquisite poetry. Costumes very rich. Scenery magnificent and expensive. Time in representation, three hours and a half. **This is a double number. Price 30 Cents.**

183 RICHELIEU; or, The Conspiracy. A Play in five acts, by Sir Edward Lytton Bulwer. An entirely new acting edition. Twelve male, two female characters. One of the most popular plays ever produced. Costumes and scenery picturesque and magnificent. Time in representation, three hours and a quarter.

184 MONEY. A Comedy in five acts, by Sir Edward Lytton Bulwer. Sixteen male, three female characters. Full of fine situations and beautiful language. Costumes modern; scenery, fashionably furnished rooms. Time in representation, three hours and a half.

185 NOT SO BAD AS WE SEEM; or, Many Sides to a Character. A Play in five acts, by Sir Edward Lytton Bulwer. An entirely new acting edition. A finely written romantic piece. Thirteen male, three female characters. Costumes of the day of Prince Charlie, the Pretender. Scenery rich; drawing room of same time. Time in representation, three hours and a quarter.

186 THE DUCHESS DE LAVALLIERE. A Play in five acts, by Sir Edward Lytton Bulwer. Six male, four female characters. Some of the acts are very powerful and emotional. Costumes costly and elegant. Scenery in palaces and convents. Time in representation, three hours and thirty minutes.

187 HIS OWN ENEMY. A Farce in one act, by the author of "The Happy Pair." Five male, one female characters. An exceedingly pleasant, witty piece. Costumes modern; scene, a handsome parlor. Time in representation, fifty-five minutes.

188 MR. X. A Farce in one act, by Sydney Rosenfeld. Three male and three female characters. An excruciatingly funny little piece, as full of life as prime Cliquot. Costumes modern; scene, a sitting room. Time in representation, fifty minutes.

189 LEAP YEAR. A Musical Duality, by Alfred B. Sedgwick. The music adapted from Offenbach's "Geneviève de Brabant." One male, one female character. Costumes modern. Scene, a handsome parlor. Time in representation, twenty minutes.

190 HUNTING THE SLIPPERS; or, Painless Dentistry. A Farce in one scene, by Martin Becher. Four male, one female characters. A rattling comic piece. Costumes modern; scene, a dentist's operating room. Time in representation, thirty-five minutes.

191 HIGH C. A Comedietta in one act (very freely adapted from the German of M. A. Grandjean), by Sydney Rosenfeld. Three male, one female characters. Very droll and sprightly. Costumes modern; scene, a well furnished room. Time in representation, forty minutes.

192 A GAME OF CARDS. A Comedietta in one act. Translated from the French by L. J. Hollenius. Three male, one female characters. So excellent is this little piece that it has been successfully played in France, Germany and Denmark. Costumes modern; scene, a handsome parlor. Time in representation, forty-five minutes.

193 MY WALKING PHOTOGRAPH. A Musical Duality in one scene. Music arranged from "La Fille de Madame Angot," by Alfred B. Sedgwick. One male, one female character. Scene, handsome parlor; costumes modern. Time in representation thirty minutes.

"Let those laugh now who never laughed before ;
And those who always laughed now laugh the more."

Nothing so thorough and complete in the way of Ethiopian and Comic Dramas has ever been printed as those that appear in the following list. Not only are the plots excellent, the characters droll, the incidents funny, the language humorous, but all the situations, by-play, positions, pantomimic business, scenery and tricks are so plainly set down and clearly explained, that the merest novice could put any of them on the Stage. Included in this Catalogue are all the most laughable and effective pieces of their class ever produced.

*** In ordering, please copy the figures at the commencement of each Play, which indicate the number of the piece in "DE WITT'S ETHIOPIAN AND COMIC DRAMA."

☞ Any of the following Plays sent, postage free, on receipt of price—fifteen cents.

Address as on first page of this Catalogue.

DE WITT'S ETHIOPIAN  COMIC DRAMA.

No.

1 THE LAST OF THE MOHICANS. An Ethiopian Sketch, by J. C. Stewart. Three male and one female characters. Costumes of the day, except Indian shirts, &c. Two scenes, chamber and wood. Time in representation, eighteen minutes.

2 TRICKS. An Ethiopian Sketch, by J. C. Stewart. Five male and two female characters. Costumes of the period. Two scenes, two interiors. Time in representation, eighteen minutes.

3 HEMMED IN. An Ethiopian Sketch, by J. C. Stewart. Three male and one female characters. Costumes modern, and scene, a studio. Time in representation, twenty minutes.

4 EH ? WHAT IS IT ? An Ethiopian Sketch, by J. C. Stewart. Four male and one female characters. Costumes of the day, and scene, a chamber. Time in representation, twenty minutes.

5 TWO BLACK ROSES. An Ethiopian Sketch, by J. C. Stewart. Four male and one female characters. Costumes modern, and scene, an apartment. Time in representation, twenty minutes.

No.

19 MALICIOUS TRESPASS; or, Points of Law. An Ethiopian Sketch in one scene, by Charles White. Three male characters. Extravagantly comical; all the parts very good. Costumes extravagant modern garbs. Scenery, wood or landscape. Time of playing, twenty minutes.

20 GOING FOR THE CUP; or, Old Mrs. Williams' Dance. An Ethiopian Interlude, by Charles White. Four male characters. One capital part for a bright juvenile; the others very droll. Costumes modern and darkey. Scenery, a landscape or wood. Time in representation, twenty minutes.

21 SCAMPINI. An anti-tragical, comical, magical and laughable Pantomime, full of tricks and transformations, in two scenes, by Edward Warden. Six male, three female characters. Costumes extravagantly eccentric. Scenery, plain rustic chamber. Time in representation, thirty minutes.

22 OBEYING ORDERS. An Ethiopian Military Sketch in one scene, by John Arnold. Two male, one female characters. Mary Jane, a capital wench part. The piece very jocose. Costumes ludicrous military and old style dresses. Scenery either plain or fancy chamber. Time of playing, fifteen minutes.

23 HARD TIMES. A Negro Extravaganza in one scene, by Daniel D. Emmett. Five male, one female characters. Needs several good players—then there is "music in the air." Costumes burlesque, fashionable and low negro dresses. Scenery, a kitchen. Time in representation, twenty minutes.

24 BRUISED AND CURED. A Negro Burlesque Sketch in one scene, by A. J. Leavitt. Two male characters. A rich satire upon the muscular furore of the day. Costumes tights and guernsey shirts and negro dress. Scenery, plain chamber. Time in representation, twenty minutes.

25 THE FELLOW THAT LOOKS LIKE ME. A laughable Interlude in one scene, by Oliver Durivage. Two male characters—one female. Boiling over with fun, especially if one can make up like Lester Wallack. Costumes genteel modern. Scenery, handsome chamber. Time in representation, twenty-five minutes.

26 RIVAL TENANTS. A Negro Sketch, by George L. Stout. Four male characters. Humorously satirical; the parts all very funny. Costumes negro and modern. Scenery, an old kitchen. Time of playing, twenty minutes.

27 ONE HUNDREDTH NIGHT OF HAMLET. A Negro Sketch, by Charles White. Seven male, one female characters. Affords excellent chance for imitations of popular "stars." Costumes modern, some very shabby. Scenery, plain chamber. Time in representation, twenty minutes.

28 UNCLE EPH'S DREAM. An Original Negro Sketch in two scenes and two tableaux, arranged by Charles White. Three male, one female characters. A very pathetic little piece, with a sprinkling of humor. Costumes, a modern southern dress and negro toggery. Scenery, wood, mansion and negro hut. Time in representation, twenty minutes.

29 WHO DIED FIRST? A Negro Sketch in one Scene, by A. J. Leavitt. Three male, one female characters. Jasper and Hannah are both very comical personages. Costumes, ordinary street dress and common darkey clothes. Scenery, a kitchen. Time in representation, twenty minutes.

30 ONE NIGHT IN A BAR ROOM. A Burlesque Sketch, arranged by Charles White. Seven male characters. Has a funny Dutchman and two good darkey characters. Costume, one Dutch and several modern. Scenery, an ordinary interior. Time in representation, twenty minutes.

No.

31 GLYCERINE OIL. An Ethiopian Sketch, by John Ar-nold. Three male characters, all good. Costumes, Quaker and eccentric modern. Scenery, a street and a kitchen. Time in representation, fifteen minutes.

32 WAKE UP, WILLIAM HENRY. A Negro Sketch, arranged by Charles White. Three male characters, which have been favorites of our best performers. Costumes modern—some eccentric. Scenery plain chamber. Time in representation, ten minutes.

33 JEALOUS HUSBAND. A Negro Sketch, arranged by Charles White. Two male, one female characters. Full of farcical dialogue. Costumes, ordinary modern dress. Scenery, a fancy rustic chamber. Time in representation, twenty minutes.

34 THREE STRINGS TO ONE BOW. An Ethiopian Sketch in one scene, arranged by Charles White. Four male, one female characters. Full of rough, practical jokes. Costumes, modern. Scenery, a landscape. Time in representation, fifteen minutes.

35 COAL HEAVERS' REVENGE. A Negro Sketch in one scene, by George L. Stout. Six male characters. The two coal heavers have "roaring" parts. Costumes, modern, Irish and negro comic make up. Scenery, landscape. Time in representation, twenty minutes.

36 LAUGHING GAS. A Negro Burlesque Sketch in one scene, arranged by Charles White. Six male, one female characters. Is a favorite with our best companies. Costumes, one modern genteel, the rest ordinary negro. Scenery, plain chamber. Time of playing, fifteen minutes.

37 A LUCKY JOB. A Negro Farce in two scenes, arranged by Charles White. Three male, two female characters. A rattling, lively piece. Costumes, modern and eccentric. Scenery, street and fancy chamber. Time in representation, thirty minutes.

38 SIAMESE TWINS. A Negro Burlesque Sketch, in two scenes, arranged by Charles White. Five male characters. One of the richest in fun of any going. Costumes, Irish, darkey and one wizard's dress. Scenery, a street and a chamber. Time in representation, twenty-five minutes.

39 WANTED A NURSE. A laughable Sketch in one scene, arranged by Charles White. Four male characters. All the characters first rate. Costume, modern, extravagant, one Dutch dress. Scenery, a plain kitchen. Time in representation, twenty minutes.

40 A BIG MISTAKE. A Negro Sketch in one scene, by A. J. Leavitt. Four male characters. Full of most absurdly funny incidents. Costumes, modern ; one policeman's uniform. Scenery, a plain chamber. Time in representation, eighteen minutes.

41. CREMATION. An Ethiopian Sketch in two scenes, by A. J. Leavitt. Eight male, one female characters. Full of broad, palpable hits at the last sensation. Costumes modern, some eccentric. Scenery, a street and a plain chamber. Time in representation, twenty-five minutes.

42. BAD WHISKEY. A comic Irish Sketch in one scene, by Sam Rickey and Master Barney. Two male, one female characters. One of the very best of its class. Extravagant low Irish dress and a policeman's uniform.

43 BABY ELEPHANT. A Negro Sketch in two scenes. By J. C. Stewart. Seven male, one female characters. Uproariously comic in idea and execution. Costumes, modern. Scenery, one street, one chamber. Time in representation, twenty-five minutes.

44 THE MUSICAL SERVANT. An Ethiopian Sketch in one scene, by Phil. H. Mowrey. Three male characters. Very original and very droll. Costumes, modern and low darkey. Scenery, a plain chamber. Time in representation, fifteen minutes.

No.

45 REMITTANCE FROM HOME. An Ethiopian Sketch in one scene, by A. J. Leavitt. Six male characters. A very lively piece, full of bustle, and giving half a dozen people a good chance. Time in representation, twenty minutes.

46 A SLIPPERY DAY. An Ethiopian Sketch in one scene, by Robert Hart. Six male, one female characters. By a very simple mechanical contrivance, plainly planned and described in this book, a few persons can keep an audience roaring. Time in representation, sixteen minutes.

47 TAKE IT, DON'T TAKE IT. A Negro Sketch in one scene, by John Wild. Two male characters. Affords a capital chance for two good persons to "do" the heaviest kind of deep, deep tragedy. Time of representation, twenty-three minutes.

48 HIGH JACK, THE HEELER. An Ethiopian Sketch in one scene, by A. J. Leavitt. Six male characters. Happily hits off the short-haired bragging "fighters" that can't lick a piece of big taffy. Time of playing, twenty minutes.

49 A NIGHT IN A STRANGE HOTEL. A laughable Negro Sketch in one scene, arranged by Charles White. Two male characters. Although this piece has only two personators, it is full of fun. Time in representation, eighteen minutes.

50 THE DRAFT. A Negro Sketch in one act and two scenes, by Charles White. Six male characters. A good deal of humor of the Mulligan Guard and Awkward Squad style, dramatized. Time in representation, eighteen minutes.

51 FISHERMAN'S LUCK. An Ethiopian Sketch in one scene, by Charles White. Two male characters. Decidedly the best "fish story" ever told. It needs two "star" darkeys to do it. Time in representation, fifteen minutes.

52 EXCISE TRIALS. A Burlesque Negro Sketch in one scene, arranged by Charles White. Ten male, one female characters. Full of strong local satire ; can be easily adapted to any locality. Time of representation, twenty minutes.

53 DAMON AND PYTHIAS. A Negro Burlesque, by Chas. White. Five male, one female characters, in two scenes. A stunning burlesque of the highfalutin melodrama ; capital for one or two good imitators. Time of representation, fifteen minutes.

54 THEM PAPERS. An Ethiopian Sketch in one scene, by A. J. Leavitt. Three male characters. Full of comical mystifications and absurdly funny situations. Time of representation, fifteen minutes.

55 RIGGING A PURCHASE. A Negro Sketch in one scene, by A. J. Leavitt. Three male characters. Full of broad comical effects. Time in representation, fifteen minutes.

56 THE STAGE STRUCK COUPLE. A laughable Interlude in one scene, by Charles White. Two male, one female characters. Gives the comical phase of juvenile dramatic furor ; very droll, contrasted with the matter-of-fact darkey. Time in representation, fifteen minutes.

57 POMPEY'S PATIENTS. A laughable Interlude in two scenes, arranged by Charles White. Six male characters. Very funny practical tricks of a fast youth to gain the governor's consent to his wedding his true love. Half a dozen good chances for good actors. Time in representation, twenty minutes.

No.

58 GHOST IN A PAWN SHOP. An Ethiopian Sketch in one scene, by Mr. Mackey. Four male characters. As comical as its title ; running over with practical jokes. Time of representation, twenty minutes.

59 THE SAUSAGE MAKERS. A Negro Burlesque Sketch in two scenes, arranged by Charles White. Five male, one female characters. An old story worked up with a deal of laughable effect. The ponderous sausage machine and other properties need not cost more than a couple of dollars. Time of representation, twenty minutes.

60 THE LOST WILL. A Negro Sketch, by A. J. Leavitt. Four male characters. Very droll from the word "go." Time of representation, eighteen minutes.

61 THE HAPPY COUPLE. A Short Humorous scene, ar ranged by Charles White. Two male, one female characters. A spirited burlesque of foolish jealousy. Sam is a very frolicsome, and very fanny young darkey. Time of playing, seventeen minutes.

62 VINEGAR BITTERS. A Negro Sketch in one scene, ar ranged by Charles White. Six male, one female characters. A broad burlesque of the popular patent medicine business ; plenty of humorous incidents. Time of representation, fifteen minutes.

63 THE DARKEY'S STRATAGEM. A Negro Sketch in one act, arranged by Charles White. Three male, one female characters. Quaint courtship scenes of a pair of young darkies, ludicrously exaggerated by the tricks of the boy Cupid. Time of representation, twenty minutes.

64 THE DUTCHMAN'S GHOST. In one scene, by Larry Tooley. Four male, one female characters. Jacob Schrochorn, the jolly shoemaker and his frau, are rare ones for raising a hearty laugh. Time of representation, fifteen minutes.

65 PORTER'S TROUBLES. An Amusing Sketch in one scene, by Ed. Harrigan. Six male, one female characters. A laughable exposition of the queer freaks of a couple of eccentric lodgers that pester a poor "porter." Time in representation, eighteen minutes.

66 PORT WINE vs. JEALOUSY. A Highly Amusing Sketch, by William Carter. Two male, one female characters. Twenty minutes jammed full of the funniest kind of fun.

67 EDITOR'S TROUBLES. A Farce in one scene, by Ed ward Harrigan. Six male characters. A broad farcical description of the running of a country journal "under difficulties." Time of representation, twenty-three minutes

68 HIPPOTHEATRON OR BURLESQUE CIRCUS. An Extravagant, funny Sketch, by Charles White. Nine male characters. A rich burlesque of sports in the ring and stone smashing prodigies. Time of playing, varies with "acts" introduced.

69 SQUIRE FOR A DAY. A Negro Sketch, by A. J. Leavitt. Five male, one female characters. The "humor of it" is in the mock judicial antics of a darkey judge for a day. Time of representation, twenty minutes.

70 GUIDE TO THE STAGE. An Ethiopian Sketch, by Chas. White. Three male characters. Contains some thumping theatrical hits of the "Lay on Macduff," style. Time of playing, twelve minutes.

71 IN AND OUT. A Negro Sketch in one scene, by A. J. Leavitt. Two male characters. A very droll, lively bit of fun. Time in representation, eighteen minutes.

72 THE STRANGER. A Burlesque Negro Sketch in one scene, by A. J. Leavitt. One male, one female characters. An extravagantly comical "take off" of Kotzebue's doleful drama. Time in representation, ten minutes.

73 THE AFRICAN BOX ; or, THE MAGICIAN'S TROUBLES. A Burlesque on the "Box Mystery," in two scenes, arranged by Charles White. Brimful of roaring fun. Five male characters. Time in representation, twenty minutes.

74 THE SLEEPWALKER. An Ethiopian Sketch in two scenes, by A. J. Leavitt. Three male characters. A cornucopia of irrepressible cacchination. Time in representation, twenty minutes.

75 WESTON THE WALKIST. A very Amusing Sketch in one scene, by John Mack. Seven male, one female characters. A capital hit at the "thousand miles in a thousand hours" mania. Time in representation, twenty minutes.

76 1, 2, 3 (or "BOUNCE"). A Negro Sketch in one scene, by John Wild. Shows a happy style of getting rid of troublesome intruders. Six male, one female characters. Time in representation, twenty minutes.

77 GETTING SQUARE ON THE CALL BOY. A Humorous Negro Sketch in one scene, arranged by Charles White. Three male characters. A capital game of "tit for tat." Time in representation, fifteen minutes.

78 THE BOGUS INJUN. A very laughable Sketch in four scenes, arranged by Charles White. Five male, two female characters. Showing the effect of introducing "ye noble savage" into drawing rooms. Time of representation, sixteen minutes.

79 BARNEY'S COURTSHIP ; or MOLLIE, DEAR. A musical interlude in one act, by Harry Macarthy. One male, two female characters. This is one of the cleverest little Irish musical pieces on the stage. Time in representation, thirty minutes.

80 SCENES ON THE MISSISSIPPI. A real (Southern) darkey sketch, in two scenes, by Buckley's Minstrels. Six male characters. Full of "de ole plantation" fun. Time in representation, twenty-five minutes.

81 RIVAL ARTISTS. A Negro Sketch in one scene, arranged by Charles White. Four male characters. Lots of fun, spiced with satire. Time in representation, eighteen minutes.

82 GOOD NIGHT'S REST. A Sketch in one scene, arranged by Charles White. Four male characters. Amusingly shows how the weary traveller is "taken in and done for." Time in representation, fifteen minutes.

83 THE GERMAN EMIGRANT. A Laughable Sketch in one scene, by Larry Tooley. Two male, two female characters. Full of funny action and humorous talk. Time in representation, twenty minutes.

84 THE SERENADE. A Negro Sketch, in two scenes, arranged by Charles White. Rich, broad humor bubbles up in every page. Seven male characters. Time of playing, seventeen minutes.

85 THE YOUNG SCAMP. A Darkey Sketch in one scene, by Add Weaver. Three male characters. The players that can't tickle an audience with this piece, had better "hang up de fiddle and de bow." Time in representation, fifteen minutes.

MANUSCRIPT PLAYS.

Below will be found a List of nearly all the great Dramatic successes of the present and past seasons. Every one of these Plays, it will be noticed, are the productions of the most eminent Dramatists of the age. Nothing is omitted that can in any manner lighten the duties of the Stage Manager, the Scene Painter or the Property Man.

NOTE.—In this list *D.* stands for Drama, *C.* for Comedy, *P.* for Play, *F.* for Farce, *A.* for Act, *m.* for male, *f.* for female.

ON THE JURY. *D.* 4 *A.* By Watts Phillips. 7 *m.* 4 *f.*
ELFIE ; or, THE CHERRY TREE INN. *D.* 3 *A.* By Boucicault. 6 *m.* 4 *f.*
THE TWO THORNS. *C.* 4 *A.* By James Albery. 9 *m.* 3 *f.*
A WRONG MAN IN THE RIGHT PLACE. *F.* 1 *A.* By Oxenford. 1 *m.* 3 *f.*
JEZEBEL ; or, THE DEAD RECKONING. *P.* By Boucicault. 6 *m.* 5 *f.*
THE RAPAREE. *D.* 3 *A.* By Dion Boucicault. 9 *m.* 2 *f.*
'TWIXT AXE AND CROWN. *P.* 5 *A.* By Tom Taylor. 25 *m.* 12 *f.*
THE TWO ROSES. *C.* 3 *A.* By James Albery. 5 *m.* 4 *f.*
M. P. (Member of Parliament.) *C.* 4 *A.* By T. W. Robertson. 7 *m.* 5 *f.*
MARY WARNER. *D.* 4 *A.* By Tom Taylor. 11 *m.* 5 *f.*
PHILOMEL. Romantic *D.* 3 *A.* By H. T. Craven. 6 *m.* 4 *f.*
UNCLE DICK'S DARLING. *D.* 3 *A.* By Henry J. Byron. 6 *m.* 5 *f.*
LITTLE EM'LY. *D.* 4 *A.* By Andrew Halliday. 8 *m.* 8 *f.*
FORMOSA. *D.* 4 *A.* By Dion Boucicault. 18 *m.* 8 *f.*
AN ENGLISH GENTLEMAN. *D.* 4 *A.* By Henry J. Byron. 9 *m.* 4 *f.*
FOUL PLAY. *D.* 4 *A.* By Dion Boucicault. 14 *m.* 2 *f.*
AFTER DARK. *D.* 4 *A.* By Dion Boucicault. 14 *m.* 2 *f.*
ARRAH-NA-POGUE. *D.* 3 *A.* By Dion Boucicault. 14 *m.* 2 *f.*
BLACK AND WHITE. *D.* 3 *A.* By Wilkie Collins and C. Fechter. 6 *m.* 2 *f*
PARTNERS FOR LIFE. *C.* 3 *A.* By Henry J. Byron. 7 *m.* 4 *f.*
KERRY ; or, NIGHT AND MORNING. *C.* 1 *A.* By Boucicault. 4 *m.* 2 *f.*
HINKO. *P.* 5 *A.* By W. G. Wills. 10 *m.* 7 *f.*
NOT IF I KNOW IT. *F.* 1 *A.* By John Maddison Morton. 4 *m.* 4 *f.*
DAISY FARM. *D.* 4 *A.* By Henry J. Byron. 10 *m.* 4 *f.*
EILEEN OGE. *D.* 4 *A.* By Edmund Falconer. 15 *m.* 4 *f.*
NOTRE DAME. *D.* 3 *A.* By Andrew Halliday. 7 *m.* 4 *f.*
JOAN OF ARC. *T.* 5 *A.* By Tom Taylor. 21 *m.* 4 *f.*
OUR AMERICAN COUSIN. *C.* 3 *A.* By Tom Taylor. 10 *m.* 7 *f.*
JANET PRIDE. *D.* Prologue and 4 *A.* By Dion Boucicault. 9 *m.* 3 *f.*
JENNIE DEANS. *D.* 3 *A.* By Dion Boucicault. 12 *m.* 5 *f.*
THE FAIRY CIRCLE. Fairy *D.* 2 *A.* 8 *m.* 4 *f.*
OUR BOYS. *C.* 3 *A.* By H. J. Byron. 6 *m.* 4 *f.*
ULTIMO ; or, MONEY AND BRAINS. By G. Von Moser. *C.* 5 *A.* 8 *m.* 7 *f.*

☞ *Manuscript copies of these very effective and very successful plays are now ready, and will be furnished to Managers on very reasonable terms.*

OPERATIC SONGS.

COMIC AND SERIO COMIC SONGS.

MOTTO SONGS.